THE THREE ASTRONAUTS

THE THREE ASTRONAUTS

UMBERTO ECO & EUGENIO CARMI

Translated by William Weaver

SECKER & WARBURG

LONDON

Once upon a time there was Earth.

And once upon a time there was Mars.

They were very far apart,
in the midst of the sky,
and all around them were millions of planets
and millions of galaxies.

The people who lived on Earth
wanted to reach Mars and the other planets,
but the planets were far away.

All the same, the people set to work.
First they launched satellites that circled Earth
for two days, then came back again.

Then they launched rockets, but instead
of coming back down the rockets escaped
the pull of Earth's gravity and went off
into infinite space.

At first they put dogs in the rockets;
but the dogs couldn't talk, and the only message
they sent over the radio was "bow wow."
And nobody could figure out what
the dogs had seen or what places
they had reached.

Finally they found some brave men who wanted
to be astronauts.

Astronauts explore the stars,
infinite space, the planets and galaxies,
and everything all around them.

They took off, not knowing if they
would come back. Because Earth
had become too crowded, and there were
more and more people on it every day,
the astronauts wanted to conquer the stars
so that one day everybody would be able
to travel from one planet to another.

One fine morning three rockets took off
from three different places on Earth.

In the first there was an American, happily
whistling a bit of jazz.
In the second there was a Russian,
singing ``The Song of the Volga Boatman.''
In the third there was a Chinese, singing
a beautiful song—though the other two thought
he was all out of tune.

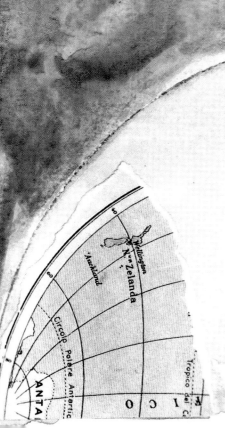

Each wanted to be the first man
to set foot on Mars, because he wanted to show
that he was the best.

It so happened that the American didn't like
the Russian, and the Russian didn't like the Chinese,
and the Chinese was suspicious of the other two.
This was because the American,
to greet somebody, said "How do you do?"
and the Russian said "Здравствуйте"
and the Chinese said "你們好."
They didn't understand one another, and each
thought the other two were peculiar.

Since all three of them were very smart,
they landed on Mars at almost the same time.
They got out of their spaceships,
wearing their helmets
and their space suits . . .

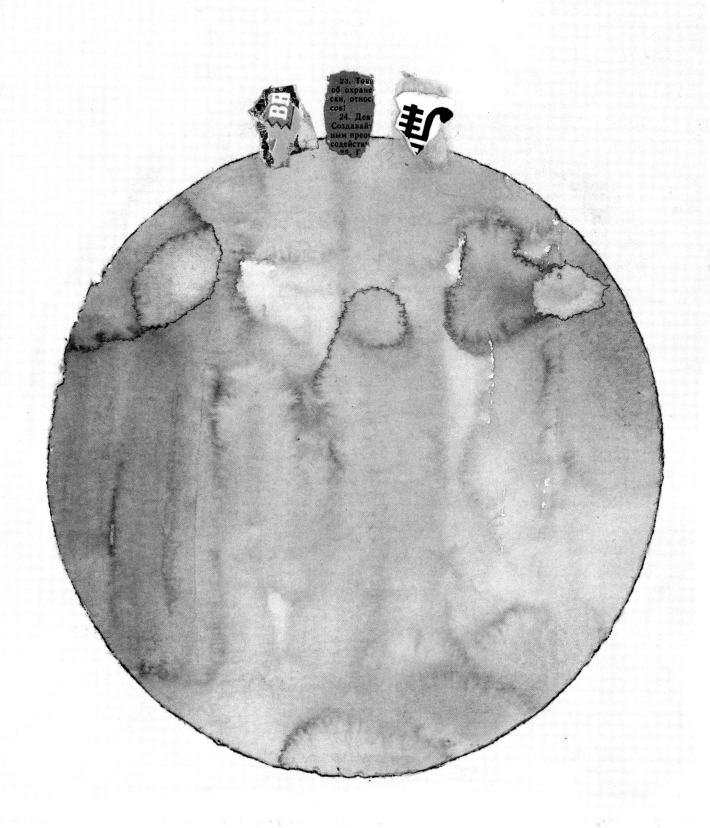

. . . and they found a marvellous and disturbing
landscape: the ground was striped
by long canals full of emerald green water.
There were trees of a strange blue with birds
such as no one had ever seen, their feathers
of an equally strange colour.

On the horizon there were red mountains that gave off eerie flashes.

The astronauts looked at the landscape. They looked at one another distrustfully. And each kept his distance.

УГРО

НЬЮ-ЙОРК, 10.
...бря в: маленьк
(...вада) должен н
...вистами антиво
...ющей за прекра
...ами ядерных исп
Статья о «престу
...кстати, не п
...н судебных

Then night fell. There was a curious silence
all around, and Earth shone in the sky as if
it were a distant star.

The astronauts felt sad and lost, and in the darkness
the American called for his mother.

``Mommy,'' he said.

And the Russian said: ``Mamochka.''

And the Chinese said: ``Mama.''

But they realized almost at once that they were
saying the same thing and feeling the same feelings.
So they smiled at one another, moved closer,
and together lit a nice little fire, and each
sang the songs of his home country.
Their spirits were raised, and, as they waited
for morning, they got to know one another.

mommy   МАМОЧКА   媽媽

Finally morning came. It was very cold.
Suddenly from a clump of trees a Martian appeared.
He was truly horrible to look at—green all over,
with a pair of antennae instead of ears,
a trunk, and six arms.

He looked at them and said: ``Grrrr!''

Which in his language meant: ``My goodness!
Who are these horrible creatures?!''

But the Earthlings didn't understand him
and believed he had uttered a war growl.

grrrr.....

He was so different from them
they weren't able to understand him or love him.
All three immediately felt like fighting him.

Now that they were faced with this monster,
their little differences vanished. What did it matter
if they spoke different languages? They realized
that all three of them were human beings.

But this other one wasn't.
He was too ugly, and the Earthlings thought
that anybody who was ugly was also bad.

So they decided to kill him
with their atomic disintegrators.

But suddenly, in the great cold of the morning,
a Martian baby bird, in leaving its nest,
fell to the ground, shivering with cold
and with fear.

It cheeped desperately, more or less like
a little bird on Earth. It was heartbreaking.
The American, the Russian, and the Chinese
looked at it and couldn't help shedding
a tear of pity.

At that moment, something strange happened.
The Martian went over to the bird, looked at it,
and puffed two jets of smoke from his trunk.

And the Earthlings, all at once, realized
that the Martian was crying.
In his own, Martian way.

Then they saw him bend over
the little bird and pick it up in his six arms,
trying to warm it.

The Chinese turned toward
his two friends from Earth.
"You see?" he said. "We thought this monster
was different from us, but he
likes animals, too, and he can cry; he has a heart,
and surely he has a brain as well!

Do you still think we should kill him?"

There was really no need to ask.

The Earthlings had learned their lesson by now:
Just because two creatures are different they don't
have to be enemies.

So each went over to the Martian,
with his hand extended.

And since the Martian had six, he could
shake hands with all three men at once and,
at the same time, he could wave joyfully
with his other hands.

And, pointing to Earth up there
in the sky, he indicated that he would
like to take a trip, to meet the Earthlings
and figure out with them the way to found
a great republic of space where everybody
could live happily ever after.

Delighted, the astronauts said yes.

And to celebrate the occasion,
they offered him a little bottle
of cool water they had brought from Earth.
Overjoyed, the Martian stuck his trunk
into the bottle and inhaled a healthy swig.
Then he announced that he liked this drink
a lot, even though it went to his head.

And so the visitors realized
that on Earth, and on the other planets, too,
each one has his ways, and it's simply a matter
of reaching an understanding.

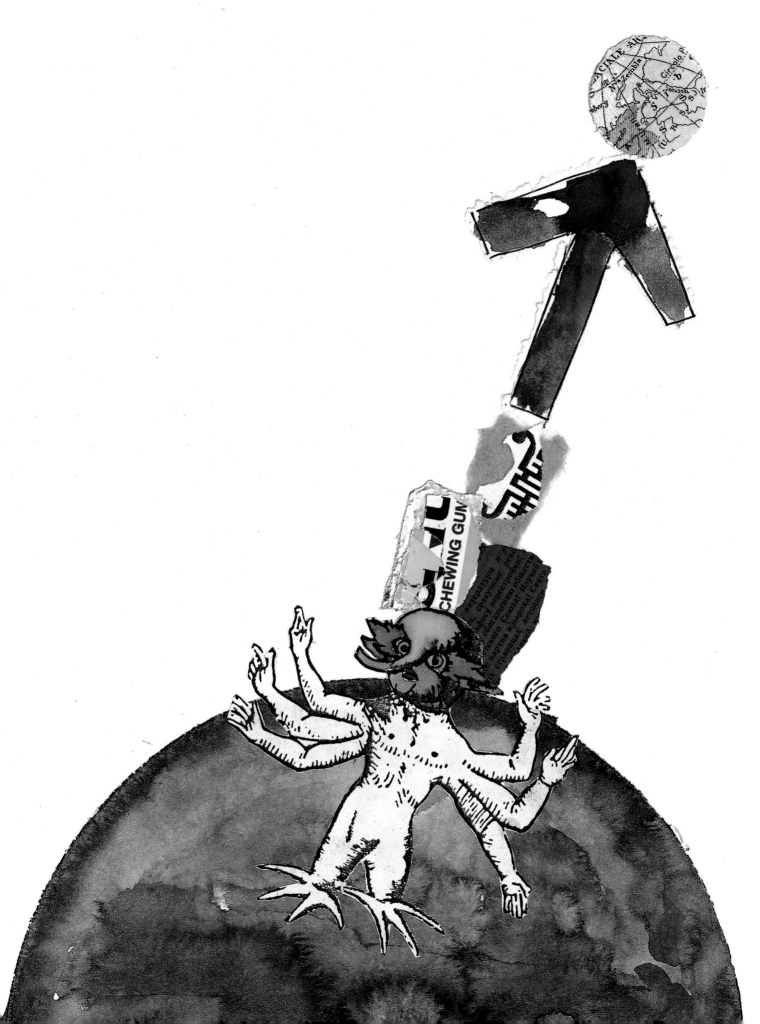

First published in Great Britain in 1989 by

Martin Secker & Warburg Limited

Michelin House, 81 Fulham Road, London SW3 6RB

Text and illustrations copyright © 1989 by Gruppo Editoriale Fabbri,

Bompiani, Sonzogno, Etas S.p.A.

English translation copyright © 1989 by Harcourt Brace Jovanovich, Inc.

ISBN: 0 436 14094 2

Printed and bound in Italy